# DRAGON WAS TERRIBLE

**KELLY DiPUCCHIO** ✳ **PICTURES BY GREG PIZZOLI**

FARRAR STRAUS GIROUX • NEW YORK

# Dragon was terrible.
Naturally, dragons have a bit of terrible in them because they're dragons after all.

But THIS dragon here?
## Super terrible.

He stomped on flowers.

He played tricks on the guards.

And he spit on cupcakes.
Who does that?!

Dragon, that's who.

That's not all. He scribbled in books.

He threw sand.

And he took candy from baby unicorns.
Honestly, that's terrible.

The king had had enough.
"Enough!" he said.

And he posted this sign:

**BRAVE KNIGHTS!**
WHOEVER SHALL TAME
THE TERRIBLE DRAGON
SHALL BE REWARDED
**WITH A GIFT!**
IT SHALL BE **A NICE** GIFT.
**YE SHALL LIKE IT!**

~ HIS ROYAL MAJESTY, THE KING

DRAGON
WAS
HERE

Knights lined up to show off
their dragon-taming skills.

They all failed. Miserably.
And Dragon just grew more terrible.

He chased fuzzy yellow ducklings around the moat.

He TP'd the castle.

And he burned every last royal
marshmallow to a blackened crisp.

The villagers had had enough.
"Enough!" they said.

And they posted this sign:

BRAVE ~~KNIGHTS!~~ **PEOPLE!**
WHOEVER SHALL TAME
THE TERRIBLE DRAGON
SHALL BE REWARDED
WITH A GIFT!
(FROM THE KING.)
IT SHALL BE **A NICE** GIFT.
(WE HOPE.)
YE SHALL LIKE IT!
(PERHAPS.)
~ HIS ROYAL MAJESTY, THE KING ♛

DRAGON WAS HERE

DRAGON WAS HERE AGAIN

Ordinary blokes and lassies lined up
to try their hand at taming the dragon.

They all failed. Embarrassingly so.
And just when you thought it wasn't possible,
Dragon grew even *more* terrible!

And he burped in church. Loudly.
Honestly, that's terrible **and** rude.

A boy wearing a feathered cap and a look of
determination had had **enough.**
Only he didn't say "Enough!"
like you thought he would.

Instead, he sketched a story.

The next day, Dragon followed
a trail of marshmallows to a shady
tree where the boy was reading.

The boy spied the dragon out
of the corner of his eye and
began to read aloud
in a booming voice.

"And then the brave dragon swooped in to save the princess . . ." he said.

Dragon stopped in his tracks.

"... but the terrible knight pulled out his wicked sword!"

Dragon pretended not to listen.

"The brave dragon ROARED and the fraidy-cat knight trembled in his boots!"

Dragon pretended to walk away.

A crowd began to gather and Dragon took cover
in a tree. The boy continued reading . . .

. . . page,

. . . after page,

. . . after page.

Until . . .

# SNAP! CRASH!
Dragon landed on the ground
with a terrible THUD.

The clever boy didn't flinch.
He reached out a hand
to the dragon and said,
"Would you like to hear how the story ends?"

And just when you thought it wasn't possible . . .

. . . Dragon smiled.

And he took a seat beneath
the tree with the other children.

Honestly, that's adorable.

The king cheered! The villagers cheered!
The baby unicorn and fuzzy ducklings
cheered the loudest of all!

At long last, the terrible dragon had been tamed.

# THE END

# HEY, WAIT . . .
## What about the reward?

Oh, yes. That.
The gift was a new friend . . .
. . . A nice dragon, of course.

For Jude, a brave knight

—K.D.

For Kelly and Janine

—G.P.

Farrar Straus Giroux Books for Young Readers
175 Fifth Avenue, New York 10010

Text copyright © 2016 by Kelly DiPucchio
Pictures copyright © 2016 by Greg Pizzoli
All rights reserved
Color separations by Bright Arts (H.K.) Ltd.
Printed in the United States of America by Phoenix Color,
Hagerstown, Maryland
First edition, 2016
3  5  7  9  10  8  6  4  2

mackids.com

Library of Congress Control Number: 2015960159

ISBN: 978-0-374-30049-4

Our books may be purchased in bulk for promotional, educational, or business use. Please
contact your local bookseller or the Macmillan Corporate and Premium Sales Department at
(800) 221-7945 ext. 5442 or by e-mail at MacmillanSpecialMarkets@macmillan.com.